Monsters, Monsters GO AWAY!!

Arthur Land

Illustrated by Jessica Warrick

Makdan
PUBLISHING
Bonney Lake, WA

Monsters, Monsters GO AWAY!!

Contact
Attn: Arthur Land
Makdan Publishing
P. O. Box 7560
Bonney Lake, WA 98391
arthurland@makdanpublishing.com

ISBN: 9780981928302

Library of Congress Control Number: 2008938119

Land, Arthur
Children's Books

By Arthur Land
Illustrations by Jessica Warrick
Cover and book design by Kiskis Designs

Makdan Publishing
P. O. Box 7560
Bonney Lake, WA 98391
publisher@makdanpublishing.com
www.makdanpublishing.com

Printed in China

10 09 08 07 06 1 2 3 4 5

For
Aidan and Makena
My own little
Monster Masters

At the Brave's house moving day has come
The boxes are packed and ready to go
There's lots of work, no time to play
But Bobby and Becky are moving very slow

Mom and Dad come into the room
New jobs and home bring only smiles
"The time has come to leave this house
We've got to drive lots of miles!!"

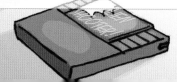

Two days of travel to their new town
Through plains and hills, ups and downs
All the way the back seat is quiet
As Bobby and Becky sit with frowns

Through Beaconville the family drives
'Til they finally reach their new place
It is dark and old and very large
And a bit of fear shows on Bobby's face

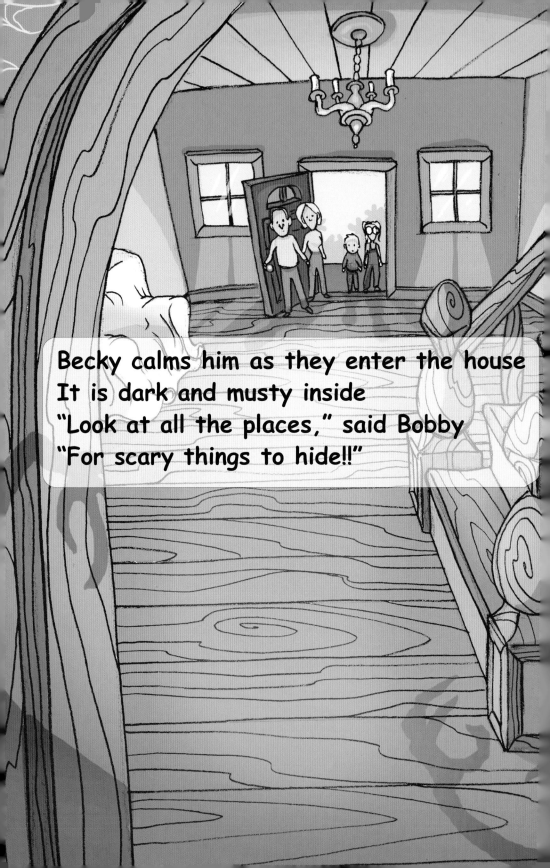

Becky calms him as they enter the house
It is dark and musty inside
"Look at all the places," said Bobby
"For scary things to hide!!"

Mom and Dad can only smile
And ignore all his fears and dread
"It's just the old and dusty webs
Any Monsters are in your head!"

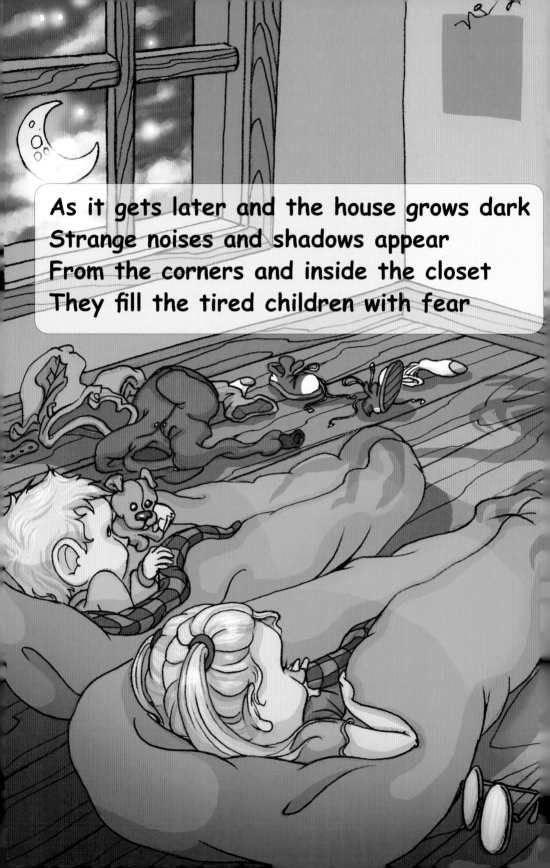

As it gets later and the house grows dark
Strange noises and shadows appear
From the corners and inside the closet
They fill the tired children with fear

The sun arose as morning came
  But the children are still very sleepy
They run downstairs to tell mom and dad
"Our first night was very creepy!!"

Down the stairs and into the kitchen
The frightened children flew
Before they speak, their parents say
"We have something for both of you!!"

As they open the door that leads outside
Into the house runs their surprise
A golden haired dog is what it is
Bobby and Becky can't believe their eyes

They run to hug their new best friend
Knightlight greets them with kisses so wet
So happy with him are Bobby and Becky
That their scary night they soon forget

Then Ms. Delancey the neighbor comes in
"She's here to look after you two"
Their parents say as they leave
To do what working parents do

As Ms. Delancey makes herself busy
Bobby and Becky decide to explore
Up the stairs the search begins
Where Bobby discovers a secret door

An attic full of treasure they find
"Let's not make too much racket"
Becky says as they search the stuff
And Bobby tries on an old jacket

"What's that there in the pocket?"
Becky asks Bobby with pleasure
They open it up and see it's a map
"I bet that it leads to some treasure!"

Brother and sister walk hand and hand
Through their big backyard they wind
With Knightlight showing them the way
The clues are not so hard to find

They follow the map, step by step
And are very excited to see
That the trail finally ends at
The crossed roots of an old oak tree

With a shovel they find the digging starts
But both get tired and want to rest
When the shovel hits something hard
Bobby and Becky find an old wooden chest

The children dig with Knightlight's help
      To free the box from the ground
When it's finally out the children shout
      "Look at the treasure we found!"

In the chest a book is packed
It's old and worn and frayed
They open it carefully and find
Names and pictures displayed

The box is filled with more secrets
Some old and worn out treasure
A doggy collar and a lantern
Bobby can't help but giggle with pleasure

As once again the night comes in
Bobby and Becky ready for bed
Scary noises throughout the house
Filling them both with dread

Monsters lurk in every shadow
They'll be no sleep tonight
They have their lantern, collar and book
And snuggle close with Knightlight

They're up at dawn, but oh so tired
And know they have to look
To see if any answers come
From inside their new found book

"Wow!" They both exclaim
"Here's a plan for Monster Mist
A spray to banish all your fears
But it's such a long, long list!"

The recipe and another map
Will guide them to what they seek
With jackets on the children go outside
And head to Courage Creek

Through the forest Bobby and Becky go
With map and book in hand
Creepy shadows are everywhere
Around this scary land

They finally arrive at Courage Creek
To fill up a canteen
And find their fears have gone away
In the prettiest place they've ever seen

Now the children have their water
Yet need more ingredients to make it best
If they want to scare the monsters away
They will have to seek the rest

Bobby and Becky go house to house
With Ms. Delancey close behind
The neighborhood kids help a lot
And the rest of the items they find

Now at night when the monsters come
They can use the Monster Mist
Made from water, branches and flowers
And everything else on their list

Inside the book there are some words
That they also need to recite
Then the Monster Mist will work
And they can have a peaceful night

That same night the children sleep
It had been such an exciting day
They sprayed the spray and said the words
And all of the monsters have gone away!!

Monster Mist Creed

Here I am inside my room
With the mist that I have made
I use it while I say the words,
And I am not afraid.

All you Monsters Everywhere
Listen to what I say
When I use this Monster Mist
Monsters, Monsters
GO AWAY!!

Monster Mist

Monsters underneath
your bed
And in your closet too?
Spray them all with
Monster Mist
Like Bobby and Becky do!

www.themonstermasters.com